A Modern Witches Guide To Traditional Witch Craft

Dedicated to my beautiful boy. Magic will live in you always x

What Brings You To This Book?

Welcome to the world of traditional magic! Are you looking for a detailed introduction to the world of witchcraft? Then you have come to the right place! In this book, we will explore the history and origins of witchcraft and spells, as well as provide detailed instructions on how to use them in your own practice. We will also discuss the different types of spells from simple charms and incantations to more complex rituals - you will find an enchantment for anything under the sun within these hallowed pages, well almost anyway.

Witchcraft and spell-casting have been around for thousands of years, and its power to bring about change is still relevant today. This spell book offers a detailed introduction to the practice of witchcraft and spells, exploring the history, rituals, tools, and techniques that witches use to cast their spells. Whether you're a beginner or an experienced practitioner, this book will help you dive deeper into the wanders of witchcraft.

So, before we begin , I simply must give you some wise words of warning.

An important thing to remember is to research - obviously - every ingredient , if you are pregnant , have allergies , have pets, have children, have underlying health conditions etc , because skin irritation or allergic reactions could aways occur.

Even when I was a child before the age of google, my mother always avoided mugwort in her spells while pregnant. So be sure to do your research.

Always have a well ventilated area. Essentially be sure to use common sense always. If a spell calls for a night woods walk, don't go alone - obviously.

We may be witches but there will always be weirdos! Being a teen witch at 13 my mother would never let me wonder into the forest past tea time. I used to really be annoyed as I wanted to have moon ceremonies amongst nature on my own. But now, I get it. It's not safe for anyone in the woods at night, let alone a 13 year old, and that goes for everything in this book. Take it with a pinch of salt (literally!) And never do anything that would seem inappropriate for you.

This book is a very powerful tool to manifest your intentions in life and manifest the things that you want in life. However, it should not be used with malicious intent as it will cause more harm than good.

Witchcraft should only be used to bring about positive change in the world, and ultimately, one must understand the consequences of their actions and take responsibility for them.

One of the most important principles of witchcraft is "What you put out, you receive back times three". This means that whatever energy or intention we put out into the universe will come back threefold - both positive and negative energy. Therefore, it's vitally important to ensure that all spells are done with good intentions when practicing Witchcraft. No spell should be done with evil in your heart or mind as this could lead you down a destructive path and bring about more chaos than balance and harmony into your life. As with all things in life, magic carries its own unique set of risks that must be properly understood before attempting to use it. Although magic is a very beneficial tool and can in turn provide great strength but it also demands an equally great price from the practitioner who engages in it. A lack of understanding or respect for the underlying forces at play within these shadowy realms may bring about untold destruction not only upon yourself, but those whom you hold most dear. Therefore caution should always be exercised when delving into such practices or even contemplating using any kind of magical rite which could potentially have undesirable consequences attached to it—especially if one plans to delve deep into darker forms or rituals initiated under duress.

Now let me tell you a little about me and why I've wrote this book.

For the last 35 years of my life, I have devoted myself to exploring and collecting magic and spells from all over the world, And in this book I have documented the most powerful spells I know. An avid follower of the occult, I have been exposed to and researched a plethora of ancient magical practices from Cambodia to Iceland. I have learned many different spells and rituals passed down to me by elder witches that practice their craft with timeless wisdom, through the practice of generational magic dating back centuries, the history and power behind these rituals evoke strong emotions that have shaped my whole life for the better. Also, The occult has been the source of fascination for me since a young age. Through generations, the practice of magic and its accompanying rituals have been passed down from one generation to the next in my family.

I was born in a small town called 'Burley' In the New Forest, Hampshire. Burley is one of the oldest occult towns in the UK with a very rich history documented around witchcraft. Every other shop in town is a witchcraft shop and we rely on most of our income from the occult tourist trade. My nans nan and her nan before her all practised with craft. I grew up watching 60's magic tv shows, In a female dominated house, Full of herbs and greenery, With the odd mini cauldron on the window sill with a protection potion stewing. All of the ladies and some of the men in my family follow the craft. So I truly feel as though i'm ready and wise enough to share my wisdom with the community of witches that surrounds us all.

It's also very important to know the origins and history that laid the foundations for witch craft as we know It today . The origins of witchcraft are still largely debated, with many theories surrounding its beginnings. It is believed to have originated in the pre-Christian era, with its practices being passed down through generations. Witchcraft has been practised for thousands of years and is often associated with other religious practices that follow the occult, such as Paganism and Wicca. These religions involve rituals and spells that are used to connect with spiritual forces, often to seek guidance or protection. Other occult practices include astrology, tarot card readings and divination. All these practices have been around for centuries and are still popular today.

Throughout the centuries, witchcraft has been heavily frowned upon and even criminalised in many societies. This is due to a number of reasons, including fear of the unknown, a lack of and understanding of the practice. Common misconceptions about witchcraft include that it is an evil practice, that it involves worshiping Satan, and that it involves casting spells and curses on people. This led to many women being falsely accused and burned at the stake for being witches. In reality, witchcraft is a spiritual practice that focuses on healing and connecting with nature.

Contrary to popular belief, witchcraft isn't something that is exclusive to a single race or gender. Anyone can become a witch, regardless of their background. Many people think that it is too complicated or too abstract to learn. However, witchcraft is not inherently difficult and anyone at any age can learn to do it. All it takes is a little knowledge, research, and commitment. It doesn't matter if you're an ancient wise woman or a modern office worker, anyone can learn to practice witchcraft and the magic it encompasses. You do not inherit power, instead you find it within yourself, we are all born with untold amount of energy inside of us, witchcraft is harnessing that energy and using it to your advantage.

Common misconceptions about witches

Throughout both folk lore and history there have been countless misconceptions about both witchcraft and witches themselves.

There are still today many people and media outlets alike that have a ridiculously skewed view of witchcraft and this view tends to come from a place of ignorance and fear. In fact, across different cultures and belief systems there are countless ways to approach magic-making and spell crafting which should be respected rather than judged harshly. So let's clear up these common misconceptions.

1) Witchcraft is not a form of satanic worship

2) Not all witches are evil and practice black magic

3) Not all witches follow Wicca

4) Witchcraft is for men and women alike

5) Witches do not eat , hunt or pray upon babies or children

6) We are not all covered in warts

7) Witches do not ride brooms

8) We are not old wrinkly hags

9) We do not eat foods like eye of newt, we much prefer a Chinese take away.

10) We do not shoot lightning from our finger tips, Yes we get it, You watched tv once. No , We don't do it.

So now we have all the formalities out of the way, let's begin.

How to Cast A Spell

Spells come in all shapes and sizes some are crazy and quirky , some are more Mundane. To cast a magic spell, you will need to prepare the necessary ingredients, tools, and ritual space. Begin by meditating to clear your mind and focus on your intention. Visualise the outcome you desire and create a mental image of it.

You can also choose to create a circle with salt or other protective herbs, and light candles or incense.

Speak your magical words out loud and visualise the desired outcome.

Finally, release the energy of the spell and close the circle.

It is customary to end a spell with the phrase *"Blessed be"*.

This phrase is used to close the spell and to indicate that the spell is complete. Its used to express gratitude to the universe or higher power for allowing the spell to take effect. Additionally, some people believe that saying "blessed be" can help to protect the spell caster from any negative consequences of the spell. I personally do believe this and me and many witches alike have been taught the importance of blessed be. It keeps the magic 'Pure' and shows good intentions to the universe.

Tools you will at

some point need :

These are basic start off bits, you'll need more and more items as your craft progresses. But these are good items to begin with. The tools you use are a lot like wine, an aged 1980 wine is going to taste a whole lot better than one brewed a week ago. The older your tools the more history and magic already runs through them.

A broom -

No not to fly around on. Firstly a broom is obviously essential for any broom spell you may cast. It is a symbol of protection and purification in magic. It is often used in rituals to sweep away negative energy and to create a sacred space.

A Cauldron -

An absolute essential. For me I also love to use my cauldron, I use a cast iron cauldron along with a silver plated cauldron and a copper cauldron . These can be found very cheaply in a charity shop, Boot-sale or even on line. Head over to an online marketplace selling second hand goods and you can pick up a vintage cauldron for £12 or less. I would always advise a second hand antique cauldron, the older the better. Then when it comes into your possession perform a cleansing spell to cleanse it of previous owners ready for yourself. However, if money is tight and you cant go out and get one right away, you can even go and use an old take away container, but in the long run, most spells will need a metal cauldron.

An athame -

Not essential but again an amazing magical tool. It's a ceremonial knife used in rituals and spell casting. It is usually made of metal and has a double-edged blade. It is used to direct energy and to symbolically cut through obstacles. Of course it is a dangerous tool so use with precaution.

A wand -

How Blasé I know. But a wand is actually very useful in spell casting, will lightning shoot out the end of it though? No not quite. A wand is used to focus and direct magical energy. It is often used to cast spells and to channel energy into rituals. The best wand you can find is a very old stick from a local woodlands. A lot of these items you'll need are always older the better .

Tarot cards -

It is personal choice if you want to use tarot or not. Some people do not like divination cards for a multitude of reason, I however, find them a very useful tool.

I often use tarot cards to gain insight into a situation, to answer questions, and to help make decisions. They're a powerful tool that can help a witch to connect with their intuition and to gain deeper understanding of the energies and influences that surround them. Additionally, the cards can be used for spell work, as a focus for meditation, and for divination.

A mortar and pestle-

Used through out the ages. Great for grinding herbs and ingredients for spells, potions, and other rituals. Also, the physical act of grinding and mixing ingredients with a mortar and pestle is often seen as a symbolic representation of the intention behind the spell or ritual, adding to its potency. You will find a lot of magical powder recipe in your items and the blender just isn't going to give the same magical potency as a mortar and pestle. Again these are easily found online, second hand and in shops. A bit expensive but if you keep an eye out you will come across a cheap one.

A spell journal-

A spell journal can be used to keep track of the ingredients and instructions used in a particular spell, as well as to document any insights or changes that were made along the way. It also serves as a personal record of the witch's magical experiences and growth, which can be a valuable resource when returning to a spell or ritual. After all what is a witch with out her spell book.

Crystals -

You will come across a thousand spells in your time that call for these. A huge help in spell casting. Crystals can be obtained in most magic and occult shops along with most markets and online, a lot of crystals are made up of mainly glass so go for a smaller crystal that is made of more crystal than glass. In this case size does not matter, It's about what's inside the crystal.

Herbs-

Again , You will always need these in spell casting. Herbs are an amazing thing. Naturally healing and unbelievably powerful and magic.

When using herbs for magic (or cooking even) they are always best to be home grown. You don't need a garden to do this nor do you need a lot of money. Herb seeds are cheap and easy to find, not so easy to sprout for beginners though. Even me a seasoned witch will prefer to buy herbs that are already sprouted, local garden centres or even DIY shops will have a range of herbs year round for a couple of pounds. Always get herbs in soil. If you treat your herbs right, they will re grow and last you a couple of years. Another amazing thing in spell work is home made oils , again you can make these by using some home grown herbs and a simple carrier oil like coconut oil. On a low heat place your herb of choice in some oil and let it stay warm (not hot) for about half an hour, the oil will turn green and will then become the herb oil of your choice.

Candles-

Do I really need to say a lot about these? Obviously you will go through a whole lot of candle whiles practising witch craft. Each candle will represent different things. You can never have enough candles. I cant stress enough how important it is to check second hand shops whenever your by one. My candle collection is very big and I've only spent the bare minimum along the way. I pick up bags of coloured candle for a pound or two in the charity shops.

How to make a potion

Again, this is where a cauldron comes in handy. Your cauldron will hold the magical energy you excude so thats why its important to pick a good one and stick with it.

For mixing I use one or two utensils and I do not change them , I simply cleanse them either at the end of the day or after a certain spell.

I have used a wooden spoon and fork that I bought in a charity shop and have used them for the last 25 years or so. When adding ingredients your usually just expected to slowly stir them while harnessing your energy into them. Some potions should be disposed of to nature or some left for a while. While you continue to practice you will start to sense just what you need to do in regards to making a potion. Potions are very very rarely ingested, most of the time they will just be for external use IE only leaving the cauldron only to be disposed off.

Who is your familiar?

Familiars which are often animals, such as cats, dogs, birds, or even reptiles. These familiars are believed to be the witches' magical helpers, providing them with supernatural powers and knowledge.

Familiars are also believed to be able to see and interact with the spirit world, allowing them to carry out rituals and spells.

I was never much of a cat person, I have always had a black bulldog since I was a young girl and have carried that on through out my life.

It is believed that some animals such as cats and owls, can have a special connection to magic and may be able to sense supernatural or magical energies, and could potentially be able to see hexes if they are powerful enough.

Magical Metals

For me personally, I believe that metals have intrinsic energy or power due to their chemical makeup or rarity, I also see them as symbols of particular elements or energies that can be harnessed for magical purposes. Additionally, certain metals can be associated with certain deities or spirits, making them significant in religious or spiritual rituals.

It's best practice not to let your bare hands come into direct contact with any form of unknown metals unless you know exactly what kind they are first. Always do a safety check on each metal before you use it.

Copper:

Copper is ruled by Venus. Associated to the letter 'I' and star sign Taurus and Libra . The Goddess Venus holds copper in high regard. Used to increase fertility and wealth.

Venus is the goddess of romance, aesthetics, the arts, harmony, balance, and peace. The planet with the slowest rotation is Venus.

Copper is a fantastic connecting material because it mixes with other metals quickly and transmits heat and energy with little effort (think of the copper in electricity wires).

Use copper in spells for affection, sensuality, friendship, healthy connections in every form, bargaining, and peace.

Gold:

Tincture of the Sun created by alchemists. Its nature is male, the Sun rules it, Leo is its star sign. The letter E, diamonds, and the heart are all represented by it.

Use for spells requiring knowledge, common sense, longevity, comfort, and money. For depression, heart comfort and fortification, hallowing, wealth, protection, and healing, use gold amulets.

Gold is typically connected with wealth, power, and truth in most civilisations.

Sun gods are associated with the male principle, power, self-assurance, creativity, wealth, investments, luck, and hope. Wearing golden jewellery might help you feel stronger and more confident.

Iron:

Associated to Aries and Scorpio, ruled by Mars and connected to the emerald and sapphire. Use as a blockade against ghosts and spirits, as well as for power, rivalry, safety, and authority.

Use iron in rituals, spells, and amulets to encourage vigour, fortitude, willpower, assertiveness, aggression, beginnings, and endeavours as well as speed, power, and bravery.

Best used in spells and amulets to promote energy, strength, determination, willpower, assertiveness and aggression, fertility rituals, beginnings and adventures, speed, strength and courage. A lot like iron rich food, making spells and potions with iron promote energy and resilience

Lead:

Ruled by Saturn, connected to Capricorn and Aquarius and associated to the spleen, the letter U and turquoise. Use for business, houses, and time.

Chronos, the Greek name for Saturn, is the father of time. Lead is his favoured metal.

For use in rituals, spells and amulets to promote contact with deep unconscious levels, deep meditation, banish negativity, quit bad habits and addictions, protect protection, stability, foundation, determination and concentration concentration

Silver:

The metal associated with the Moon, believed to be a powerful protection against negative energies and it can be used to amplify lunar magic. In astrology, Silver corresponds to crystals and the letter A . Associated to star signs Cancer which represents motherhood, family life, nurturing energy and sensitivity.

The power of silver lies in its reflective properties and its ability to absorb energy from other sources including moonlight. When charged under a full moon it can become an incredibly potent tool for magic work as well as providing a protective shield from unwanted influences.

Helps with hormones, enhances physic abilities and over all life stability.

Magic Colours

Colour is often associated with different energies, emotions, and elements, and play an important role in spell work and rituals

Red is a colour that evokes passion, courage and strength. It represents intense emotions such as love, sexual emotions and physical energy. Red also represents health, willpower and determination to succeed in life.

Yellow is a colour associated with intellect, inspiration, imagination and knowledge. Those attracted to yellow often possess the ability for clear thinking which allows them to make sound decisions when faced with difficult choices.

Green symbolises growth , wealth , renewal , balance prosperity employment fertility health luck . Green encourages us to take action on our goals dreams aspirations while still being mindful of consequences.

Blue stands for peace truth wisdom protection patience healing psychic ability harmony home understanding. People attracted to blue nurture others, provide comfort and are sensitivity

White indicates innocence, illumination , purity ,cleansing ,clarity ,establishing order, spiritual growth, understanding. It's a fluid colour that can be used in magic for almost any purpose.

Black Indicates
Dignity ,force ,stability ,protection, banishing/releasing negative energies, transformation, enlightenment.

It also signifies clouded judgement or bad intentions.

Silver stands for wisdom ,intelligence, memory ,spiritual development. Great for warding off negativity. A potent and powerful magic colour

Gold shows inner power, strength ,success ,self worth, achievement ,divine connection, creativity, expression, joy ,beauty and an inner glow. A god and goddess colour. Good for a gift to the gods.

Spells and Potions For Love

A love spell is a form of magic used to bring about desired romantic feelings, usually between two people.

The purpose of casting a magic love chant is ultimately up to each individual practitioner; however it could be said that its main purpose is generally intended for attracting one's true soulmate into his/her life; heal broken relationships; gain back lost loves; reunite estranged couples etc.

A spell for finding true love

Moon phase: Full

Materials: One Red Candle, One Red Rose, One Red Lipstick

Focus your mind and envisage what you want to gain from this spell.

Light one red candle, cover your lips in red lipstick and take one large petal from a red rose and kiss it with your lip stick covered lips , envisage you kissing the love of your life.

When the moon is full , outdoors under the light of the moon chant loudly.

By the power of love, I call upon the forces of attraction to bring true love my way. I invite the energy of love to fill my heart and life with joy, peace, and harmony. I ask that the perfect person for me appears in my life and that our connection is strong, deep, and everlasting. So mote it be!

Burn the rose petal completely while chanting.

Chant until your heart is fulfilled, slowly fading out of volume. Keep your mind focused and blow out the candle.

A spell to make your crush reciprocate your feelings

Moon Phase: Any

Materials: A photo of your crush, Rose Quartz, 1m of pink Ribbon , Pink rose petals, One Pink Candle

Take a bath in some of your pink rose petals, Clear your mind and focus solely on the person you want to fall madly in love with you. When your out of the bath and feel refreshed, sit calmly at your alter, light the pink candle and envisage what you want to gain from this spell.

Take the photo of your crush and place a rose quartz on top of it and slowly start to wrap the ribbon around it binding the quartz to the photo. Envisage yourself as the quartz and the ribbon as the love keeping the two of you tightly entangled while you fall deeply in love with each other. While doing so chant these words repeatedly

Persons Name love is what I desire

A love that binds us, strong and sure, A bond that's never meant to break.

A love like an ever-burning flame, A steady and unwavering light.

We are bound together by our love, A bond that's ever growing strong.

Repeat this chant while slowly binding the quartz to the photo. When the whole photo is bound up put it on your alter and blow out the candle. Only unwrap the photo when the spell has worked.

A Spell and potion to make your ex / old flame crave for you back

Moon Phase: Waining Crescent

Materials: Paper , Ink pen , White string , A belonging or photo of your ex (belongings are more powerful)

Under the light of the moon find a field or garden with yellow flowers, walk barefoot through the field and carefully pick a small bunch of flowers, leave an offering in exchange for the flowers. Take them home and go to your alter , clear your mind and write the name of your ex with an ink pen on paper and wrap it into the bouquet of flowers along with an item of theirs and place it in your garden and chant

The powers that be bring *Persons name* Back to me

A Ritual to know if a love will last

Materials: A sack of sunflower seeds

This old French ritual was taught to me by a lady in France in the 90s

She used tournedos flowers aka sunflower seeds

You should plant the seeds in the shape of a heart

It should be planted near lavender

If the sunflowers bloom and grow so will your love, if they do not grow or die quickly, so will your love…..

A spell to be irresistible

Materials: An outdoor spring/suitable swimming area, Flowers of all colour, Cheese Cloth, Amethyst , Red string

When the moon is shining, Find an outdoor spring or natural water swimming area ie a lake. Find and gather flowers and place them on the cheese cloth.

Take some flowers and put them in your hair and leave 3/4 quarters on the cheese cloth, Add the amethyst , Bunch it up and wrap it at the top so the flowers and crystal are secure in the cheese cloth. Strip naked and enter the water up to breast level. Clear your head and envisage your self glowing brightly in the water from a birds eye view. Dip the cheese cloth into the water and soak your head and face while chanting

I am radiant and divine, My beauty and power are undeniable. I will shine

Keep repeating these words and then very slowly start to walk out of the water while continuing to clean your body with the flowers and crystal. By the time your out of the water all of your body should have been washed with the cheese cloth.

When you arrive back home do not bath for as long as you can help for optimised results

Another spell for finding love

Moon phase: First Quarter

Materials Red Candle, A music sheet (older the better) , A red pen

A more intricate spell translated from finish. Taught to my great grandmother who used to tell us this spell for our school crushes. Start by lighting the candle at your alter. Once ready begin visualising what kind of person would make an ideal partner; envision their face and traits like hair colour etc. Take a red pen and write down on the music sheet what you see and feel for this person, Then chant aloud three times

I call upon my highest self/spirit guides/guardian angels (or whatever spiritual force resonates most with you)

please grant me perfect union with my soulmate

Now focus all energy onto finding someone who fits those criteria perfectly until feeling confident enough Fold up the paper as small as possible and pour the candle wax all over it to seal it.

Place the sheet in a bush very deeply into the bush, In Finland, they will use Viburnum opulus, commonly known as Guelder Rose but in the uk and us you can use either The Butterfly Bush (Buddleja davidii) or if not a Rose bush. Make sure you do this spell at night.

A spell to help someone find love

Materials: Jasmine, Lavender, Rose petals

This ritual is designed to open up your friend's heart and mind so that they may attract the perfect partner for them.

Begin by having them sit in a comfortable position with their eyes closed and take some deep breaths until they are relaxed. Once relaxed, ask them to visualise themselves surrounded by pink light , this will represent unconditional love from the Universe which will guide them on their quest for true love.

Have your friend mix together equal parts of rose petals , lavender and jasmine. They should then put these herbs in an airtight container or bag that has been blessed under a full moon, preferably during an eclipse or solstice period when energies are at peak power levels! Finally ask your friend to carry this bag around with him/her wherever they go as it will act as a talisman of sorts; attracting potential partners who share similar values & goals as theirs into his/her life path naturally over time without any effort whatsoever on his/hers part...

A Potion to draw in your soul mate

Materials needed: Rose petals, honey (or sugar), lavender essential oil or extract, dried chamomile flowers, pink Himalayan salt, Seeds of your choice

I founded this Soul mate Potion while in holland, shown to me by a very interesting man (his house house was covered in grass)

It has the power to draw in positive romantic energy and provide an opportunity to manifest love. To start off the ritual portion of creating this potion gather any crystals that resonate with you such as Rose Quartz or Amethyst. Place everything on your altar space (not the seeds) before beginning the next step which involves setting an intention; what specifically do you want from this spell? Is there someone special whom you wish could be attracted towards yourself? Or are simply hoping to attract more loving people into your life overall ? Take some time here by focusing deeply on what it is exactly that would make you feel most fulfilled when it comes down finding true connection .

Once ready move onto mixing up all ingredients within your cauldron (copper or silver will be best for optimised results). Add all materials in one by one while visualising how each ingredient will help draw close whatever type of relationship desired. When everything is added slowly stir while chanting

love come closer now I call thee forth

Repeatedly until done stirring , then place mixture aside still keeping focused upon same intent. Now light up chosen candles chanting those words again

Then take few deep breaths inhaling oxygenated air while feeling relaxed & present within moment at hand followed by blowing out flames once finished chanting aloud 3 times over again .

Finally pour mixture inside glass jar and leave it as an offering , it must be left out in a nature garden filled with natural elements, and lay out the seeds along with the glass jar.

This is a favourite of mine.

A Potion for Love

Moon Phase: Half moon

Material needed: Honey, Lavender oil, Rose petals

This potion is simple yet powerful. Clear your mind and envisage the type of love you crave. Whisper under your breath what they look like, smell like, talk like... go into details while making this potion.

Take one cup of honey and place it in a cauldron of your choice. Add a half cup and rose petals and 10 drops of lavender oil, slowly mix all three ingredients together until they form an even paste-like consistency then slowly add a cup of hot water and do not stir again. Do this while still describing out loud what you envisage.

Once complete, take your prepared potion outside under moonlight while focusing intently on what kind of partner you would like in your life - be sure not drink any yourself! Instead offer it up as an offering by pouring it out onto grassy areas nearby where wildlife may come across its magical properties later on during their travels throughout nature's realm .

Do not wash your cauldron until the next day.

A spell to keep your partner loyal

Materials needed: Red clover, yarrow root ,bay leaves, sandalwood chips ,hibiscus petals rosemary ,lavender, A Blue Candle, A Blue Cloth and blue string.

The idea of using magic to keep your partner loyal in a relationship is an old one. Although if someone is going to cheat, they're going to cheat, so always remember that.

I found this spell very useful to keep an eye from wandering and for them to only want you when it comes to their sexual desires.

 In your cauldron add rosemary ,lavender, red clover, yarrow root ,bay leaves, sandalwood chips ,hibiscus petals and nutmeg powder, Stir together but do not grind, just mix it up.

Transfer this mix into your blue cloth and roll it up so the contents are secure (it should look a bit like a tortilla wrap) then bind together with the blue string while chanting

Loyalty bind us together

Finishing by dripping some blue wax onto it.

Take it to the a garden or place of nature a bury it beneath either a Gladiolus, Violet or Primrose bush

A spell to get your partner to propose

Materials needed: Rose Bud, Chamomile, Honey, Basil, White and/or Red and/or Pink candles

Put the ingredients into a pot and mix them up. Leave by the light of the moon. Light some candles around yourself while holding onto either something belonging to them or even just their picture if nothing else works; visualise them proposing marriage

Lightly whisper these words

Bring me the one I seek, Let my beloved propose to me, This very week

Then offer your loved one a bath, and place the mixture into there bath and allow them to soak peacefully for an extended time

A spell to make your crush dream of you

Materials needed: Saint johns wart

Are you ready for some spy action? Ok I said spy not stalker, so please do not break in to your crushes home for the next spell. This probably works best if your friends with your crush and have access to there space. This not only makes your crush dream of you, but it keeps you in there mind all day.

Take saint johns wart to your alter and chant

Now I lay me down to sleep, My dreams of you I will keep. They light my way and make me smile, While I dream of you all the while

Then switch to

And now you lay down to sleep, your dreams of me you will keep. I will light your way and make you smile, While you dream of me all the while

Keep one sprig of the saint johns with you where you sleep and then take the other sprig and place it hidden away near where your crush sleeps.

A spell to heal a marriage

Materials: One red candle, One purple candle, A love heart spared container with a lid

Light the two candles, Take one lock of both parties hair, Put it in the love shape container. Imagine any stress, doubts or problems fading away, imagine both parties are listening and seeing each other clearly, imagine your happy future together. Pick up both candles and cross them over in your arms, Start to drop the wax from both candles onto the locks of hair while chanting

Return to love and joy and peace, that binds me and you. Let us put aside our pride, and let our love be true, Let us fill our hearts with grace, and be as one a new

Chant this until your satisfied and continue to cover the hair until 99% covered. Then add the lid and continue to drip wax over the container as if to seal it shut. Bury the container near somewhere in nature with beautiful red and purple plants.

A spell to absolutely love your self

Materials: Sea salt, Rose petals, Lavender essential oil, Chamomile tea bags (or loose leaf), One white candle

Gather these things together near your tub or shower area then take off any jewellery that may interfere with this process such as rings or necklaces before getting into the water itself. Once inside begin by lighting up your white candle while saying out loud *"I am worthy of my own love"* three times followed by taking deep breaths while focusing on what makes you unique and special - even if those qualities are small ones like having being able to make someone smile when they need it most or knowing just when someone needs a hug without them asking for one! After doing this add 1 cup of sea salt into the running water along with 3 drops each lavender essential oil & chamomile tea bags/loose leafs; stirring everything together until completely dissolved within said liquid before finally adding handfuls of rose petals throughout too!

Afterwards spend at least 15 minutes soaking in this mixture allowing its healing properties wash over both body & soul alike; imagining away any negative thoughts about oneself replacing them instead positive affirmations such as *"I am beautiful/ handsome"* , *" I deserve happiness"* etcetera until feeling contentment from within overall afterwards draining away all contents prior exiting from said space afterward drying off normally . Finally blow out flame from previously lit candle concluding entire ceremony altogether !

By using these steps regularly anyone should eventually start seeing their worthiness increase significantly overtime leading towards greater levels both confidence & inner peace than ever before ; proving once again why self love truly matters more than anything else combined

Easy Love Rituals

To have luck in attracting the opposite sex more easily, bathe with bay leaves and ginger.

Attract love to your door - If you are expecting a visitor you want to be attracted to you, grind marjoram, holly leaves and thyme and sprinkle it at the foot of the threshold they walk through

To keep your relationship happy bless rose oil and put some on your partners side of the bed

Age old magic says if a woman puts a sprig of rosemary in her hair, then the man she loves will come to her.

Blessing , Protection and Cleansing spells

A blessing spell is a type of spell used to bring divine protection and good fortune to a target. It is typically used to bring luck, protection, and overall positivity to the target. While blessing spells can be performed alone, many people find it beneficial to perform them with friends or family, in order to amplify the power of the magic and create a sense of unity and harmony

A basic blessing spell

Light your incense and chant

I cleanse this space of all negative energy and bring in protection and love

You can do this is any area and on any object that may need cleansing

A Spell to bless yourself or someone around you

Materials: White Candle (tea light) , White feather

Clear your mind and think only of positive thoughts, then light the candle.

Hold the feather and spread your hands palms up. Imagine bright light and crisp air surrounding you. Continue to do this until you feel lifted and light.

Blow out the candle. If this spell is for you leave the feather on your altar (even better if the moons light is reaching your altar)

If this ritual is for someone else, Give them the feather to carry with them for a while.

A Potion to Bless and Cleanse your home

Moon Phase: Half moon

Materials: White candles, Clear vessel (to symbolise north, west , south and east) , Lavender, Sage, Sea salt, White rice

Firstly light the candles at your altar, then take your clear vessel, This could be a drinking glass or a jar. And begin to infuse all the herbs in the salt.

Start with adding the salt into the jar with your fingers, When you are filling the jar imagine the salt signifying purity, and how you want your home to begin completely pure. Then add sage, For good vibes and clean energy.

Add Lavender to peace and tranquillity.

(Remember we're doing this slowly and imagining what each separate ingredients purpose is)

Lastly we add the white rice into the jar for abundance and prosperity.

You can do this in one jar or a couple for each place in your home.

Place these jars where people and energy enter your home. Growing up there would always be one of these jars by the front and back door, One by a window in each room, Even one when you went into the greenhouse.

They smell amazing also which is always a bonus.

Brush away the negativity

When the birds are singing take your broom and preform both a cleansing and protection spell. Sweep your whole house room my room taking it right out to the front door. This will completely cleanse your house of negative emotions bought in and also negative energy focusing towards you. Do this weekly as a great way to keep your home happy and protected

A Spell to make a wish

Materials: A Large bottle of spring water , A sunflower

Locate the largest sunflower you can find as local as possible, even if this means buying one to grow. On a blessed and starry night take your cauldron and add two cups of spring water and slowly tear the petals off the flower and add them to your cauldron while chanting

My wish is granted, I'm whole again, My joy is found, it will remain, A wish that's true, a wish that's free, My wish is granted, blessed be

While chanting and tearing off the flowers, imagine your dream coming to life.

Once the spell is finished with, empty the water into a warm bath with nothing in it apart form tap water and take a bath in the water while imagining your wish coming to life

Ocean water hex breaking spell

Moon Phase: Waining Crescent

Materials: Ocean water, A Black candle, A white cloth, A metal jar or tin (water tight)

This spell is only to be used in a circumstance your absolute sure you have been cursed or hexed. You should perform a protection spell before this and after this. You need to be on the shore, beach, or closest salt water source while casting. Do not go home to cast. Gather ocean water in a metal water tight tin, close the lid. Lay out your white cloth, Place the tin of water on the white cloth. Place the candle on top of the metal tin. Its very important to cast this spell with a clear mind and strong intent of clearing the hex from your life.

Light the candle and chant

I cast out this hex, I set these energies free. Nothing that is not meant for me, Come back to thee. Reverse this spell, I break this curse. No harm will befell, As I make it disperse, I cast away this hex, I break this curse

Repeat this and ask the gods to hear your plea. When the candle is burning , very carefully fold the cloth inwards as if to bind the tin shut with the wax and then continue to let the candle drip down and seal the tin. When the candle is about to go out, throw the tin as far out as you can. Wait for a bit, if it comes back in you need to do it again.

A spell to protect treasured belongings

Maybe your going on holiday and don't want to loose your case, or maybe your nice new car is on show In your not so nice neighbourhood. Whatever materialistic item it is you want to protect, this spell is the one for it!

Take some hore hound to your altar and chant

Fend off the evil eyes, That may try to despise, This previous thing of worth

Keep it safe and sound, Lest it be lost and found

Put the hore hound in or near your treasured item

A spell to protect a loved one

Materials: Silver coins

This spell invokes protective energy around your loved ones, this works on both family and pets, livestock etc. Slowly take the silver coins and place them in a circle around the person or animal you wish to protect. Clear your mind, set intention and walk around them while you chant

I cast this circle three times round, May no harm come near thee dwell

keep all dangers far away bound

Once you feel satisfied take the coins and place them into a blue bag. If your casting on a human give the person to the coins to hold onto. If your casting on an animal keep the coins (safely out of there reach) by near wear they sleep - you can also do that with a human too.

A Protection charm

At your alter place garlic , rosemary and 1/4 chopped onion into a hessian sack or similar and hang it by entry points in your home

A potion to rid hostility and negativity from your home and life

Take your mortar and pestle at your altar and add Sea salt, Cumin and if available Juniper. Grind and sprinkle around your windows and doorways

A Powder for peace and luck

Taught to me by my dear friend from Ireland. Take your mortar and pestle at your altar and add lemon balm, sea salt, rice, a blue flower of choice.

Grind into a powder and sprinkle in a horse shoe shape at your front door. Leave for the wind to take. If you live in a flat, Do this on your balcony / Window sill.

Salt cleansing and blessing powder

Place one whole container of table salt (cheapest version works just as well) in to your cauldron , add finely chopped sage and bay leaves. Leave it under the light of the moon until the morning. The next morning in a home that feels clean and tidy for you, transfer the mix into a clear glass bowl and leave it in the busiest room of your house for a week. When finished with bury it in a deep dark area away from your home. Do this every two months or three.

A ritual for an egg cleanse

An egg cleanse is a ritual that has been practiced for centuries in many cultures and religions. It's a very powerful way to cleanse and protect oneself from negative or evil energy.

Fill your cauldron with salty water and lemon juice

Take the egg and place it in the cauldron for a while to cleanse

Remove the egg and dry it in a clean peace of your clothing while setting your intention with the egg

Rub the egg down wards along your forehead, eyes, ears,mouth,nose etc

Carry on going down covering as much of your body as you can.

Crack the egg into a glass of Luke warm water.

Let the egg settle and read your egg

Red egg Or bad smell means you could be poorly or bad luck is nearing upon you

Veins or Shockwaves in the egg whites means you have someone physically interfering with your life and your chances of success (aka as my daughter would say you have a serious hater)

Clear water means your fully cleansed

A Spell to counter magic:

Moon Phase: New moon

Materials: Sage

This is an age old spell and often used, normally to counter spells of novice witches who had a touch of what my mother used to call 'power jealousy'.

Although the power may not yet be as strong as yours, you should give this magic a touch to invade your space. Burn sage in your metal cauldron with all windows of the house open and chant

Power of the gods, Bring strength and protection, Let no magic remain, Let all evil be gone

Repeat this chant three times, imagine the negative energies leaving and being replaced by positive energies. Take some moments to clear your mind and leave an offering on your window to nature

Another Spell to counter magic

Materials: Wooden scrubbing brush , Copal, A metal bucket (plastic will do but metal works better) rosemary and a small cedar wood stick

This spell is better to counter spells made upon others in your family or friends

At night, Take your bucket and fill it with hot water, Copal and rosemary and leave outside by the moons light. Then return into your home and open some windows, light the cedar stick and (very carefully) smudge your home, focus also on the wardrobes or whoever your keep yours and your loved ones clothing.

Lightly chant

Let the dark magic be undone, Let the shadows be gone, Let the light of love shine, Let the witch's spell be no more

When the stick has either burned out or gone out, go and get your water and preform a blessing on your scrubbing brush. Then begin to clean your front door and every door in the house with the water while again, chanting the words above.

Casting an invincible sphere

Moon phase: Waining

Materials: Sea salt , Baking soda, a glass of water, lavender oil, Olive oil, a sage plant

An intricate spell. This sphere will protect you from all spells and potions that try to penetrate it. Once the sphere is in place, it can make other peoples magic on your completely docile. The spell will continue to function for as long as a matter of weeks. Casting a sphere or as some people know it a 'Magical shield' is a very powerful spell and must be handled with caution. When cast, it allows other witches to become completely defenceless to your power , so it is important not to abuse it! Remember to read our words of warning!

Start by running a hot bath and add sea salt and baking soda, when enter it and take the glass of water with you. Spend at least one hour in this bath. Dry your self with a white towel. Now light your candle and add sea salt, and a few drops of lavender oil to your cauldron then add your olive oil on top, there should be a layer oil and a layer of liquid

While chanting

beseech ye, gods of all planes, heed my call. I summon thee and ask you to form around us a sphere of impenetrable force, and allow none to pass through unbidden. Grant us this boon for the time we require it, or until I see fit to dismiss this spell

And leave your cauldron on your alter by moon light over night. Then in the morning empty the mixture onto your sage plant and leave it in your garden / balcony

Easy Cleansing

Not everything needs an advice routine.

If someones feeling poorly, brain fog, low vibrations etc you will probably have something in your fridge to help!

Chop a large onion into 4 large pieces and place around the person with the flu, onion is a great cleanser

You can take a bowl of rice and leave it in your room for a week, it will help alleviate brain fog, negative thinking and mood swings

You can place burning oils, Orange, Pink grapefruit and lime into a burner to create an atmosphere of blessedness

On a family holiday many moons ago in India we learned a great way to bring good luck in your house hold. Boil milk on your oven and let it boil over. Of course do not leave unattended.

Place a clear jar, glass or bowl of vinegar in an area that has recently had negative energy in it to cleanse the space

Growing rosemary , thyme and sage on the window and garden words off bad energy

Take a small hessian bag, fill with fennel, stick in your letterbox to protect from evil

If your worried bad luck is approaching your home lay a line of salt across the doorway to keep them from entering

Mixing vinegar with lemon and baking powder isn't just a great way to clean, its an age old tradition to keep your house clean form bad luck. You should

When you and a loved one have an argument in the house you should take a bamboo plant and leave it in that area alone. It will act like a sponge and absorb all of the bad intentions and energy in that area.

To stop gossip spreading add a tea spoon of blessed thistle to your bath. Zen your self and centre your inner being, thinking about how your washing a wall between you and the gossip

Bathing in four leaf clovers aids your luck in many ways. A very ancient practice to ward of negative energy and also to bring about luck your way

To bring luck while your practising your craft, sprinkle nut meg on your altar

Keep a piece of birch wood by your bedroom door to stop nightmares

An enchanted gambling powder consists of sandalwood power and black pepper with just a tiny sprinkle of ginger

Money And Prosperity Magic

The goal of Money and Prosperity Magic is to help individuals manifest wealth, abundance, and success in their financial lives, whether that means attracting more money, finding new sources of income, or improving their overall financial situation.

A spell to make your business thrive

Materials: Blue candle , A paper from your business, Frankincense incense

On a Tuesday while the moon is out, take your candles and light them both at your altar. Light your incense and hold your business paper over the intense burning, Imagine the smoke coming up to cleanse the paper (your business) of any failure it may incur. Think only of the future, not the past when casting this.

My business will be successful, I'll ensure that it succeeds, I'll make it something special, with the time and the care it needs

When you feel happy with your casting, blow out your candy and return the documents to its rightful home.

A Spell For prosperity

Moon phase: Waxing or Full

Materials: Green candle

To begin, light a green candle and visualise a bright and abundant future.

As you do this, chant the affirmation of abundance

Wealth and success flow to me

Clear your mind and visualise exactly what you want to gain from this spell

When you're finished, blow out the candle and thank the universe for its blessings.

A Spell for succeeding in your career

Materials: Green incense, Note of money, A Coin (older the better) , Pen, Half a lemon , Three Sage Leaves, Green String, Honey (more local the better)

A salty spell for success at work. A very old and well known spell, everyone has their own way of casting it. I use the way my family have cast it for many years, back before it was custom for women to go and work, my nan would tell me stories of how my great grand father would cast this spell in order for him to work his way up the ladder quicker as an apprentice black smith, which in all fairness he did as with in three years he ended up taking over the whole business.

Anyway, Back to it. This is a more intricate spell, It is okay for beginners to use but make sure you go over it a few times before casting.

Firstly you need to light your incense. Then you will chant

My career is an abundance of success, I am successful in my career

Draw a circle with your pen on a note of money and place a coin on the middle of the circle.Lift the note up at either end and hold it over the smoke of the incense

Chant

I cleanse everything thats in my way

Then take your half lemon and squeeze it over the note while saying

There is purity in my intention. Satisfy my wishes.

Lastly, Take the three sage leaves and make a tiring shape around the coin that is places on the note.

I will have luck on the ladder of success

Roll the note up with coin and leaves inside and place it into your glass jar.

Fill the jar with honey and do it up, then wrap the jar around (especially near the lid) with the green string. Then continue to chant slowly

My career is an abundance of success, I am successful in my career

Until the incense burns out. Once the incense has finished, Take your jar to a green garden full of nature and flowers and bury it deeply in the soil of a green plant/bush.Also leave an offering for the universe after doing so.

Johns Money Ball

Materials needed: High John root, Basil, Paper, green thread

Wrap the high John root in basil. Fold the paper around the roots and leaves, wrap the whole of the item in green thread leaving some overage on the thread for the ball to swing.

You can swing this ball while reciting a money making chant or hang it over the door of your business to bring in custom

A spell to win a competition

Materials: Ashwagandha root, A Lilly, A hessian bag

I picked this up in Africa. I have used it myself and always found the effects to be helpful. Take the Ashwagandha root and place it in your cauldron along with the leaves from a Lilly. Loosely translated, Chant

My ambition is like a burning flame, My will shall never be tamed. I am the one who will rise to the top, I will never ever be outdone or drop

Leave the cauldron over night in the moons light and then put it into a hessian bag take it with you to whatever it Is your trying to win.

A spell to make you come into money

Materials needed: Green candle , Dried mint, a piece of gold (jewellery will work) , green plant pot, soil from a local source

Light the candle at your alter and sprinkle the dried mint around the candle, focusing on your intention for financial abundance. Then take the piece of gold and hold it in your hand and focus on the energy of abundance and prosperity flowing into your life. Place the gold down and take your empty plant pot. Place the gold at the bottom

of the plant pot, over it with the soil
while chanting

*Money grow on trees, Abundance flows
to me, Prosperity and wealth, Come to
me, by my own self*

Imagine the gold growing into a tree full
of riches. Once you've covered the gold
place it on a window sill. Take some mint
from the alter that you have sprinkled
around the candle and place it on top of
the soil. Boo out your candle before
once again chanting the above words.

Texas cedar wood oil is amazing to attract money and wealth

Growing fenugreek in your garden promote prosperity and wealth

In india practicing witches will boil brown sugar with the left over skin from oranges in a pan to attract money

Old wives tales from the south of England say wearing a green ribbon in your hair to work will keep you on a course away from poverty

Psychic Magic

Psychic magic is a form of magic that uses the power of the mind, or psychic energy, too manifest desired outcomes. You do not have to be psychic to use this kind of magic. By learning how to harness our own personal energies we become better equipped at creating positive changes within ourselves which will ultimately lead us closer towards our goals than ever before! This type of magic can be used both proactively (to bring about something new) or reactively (to undo negative patterns). Ultimately though its up to each individual practitioner what they wish their practice/ritual/ceremony looks like.

Hear others thoughts spell

On waining moon sit in a field full of purple flowers, think clearly of that you wish to gain form this spell and think clearly of your reading a person mind like a pair of lips. Recite this incantation

To hear the truth,But not to find,Hear my words,And take my time, I listen to the thoughts , Inside your mind And hear them clearly , Our thoughts are aligned

A ritual for telepathy

Begin by meditating for a while, visualise your third eye opening widely

Envisage your self walking towards a stone wall

You push the wall with your hands but it doesn't work, you continue to push to no avail

You listen to your minds eye and push instead using only your mind

The wall falls down

You are in a void floating, white lights surround you.

You are lightly drifting and floating though space and time

You hear your name getting clearer, 3 times.

Its the lights taking to you

You listen carefully to what they say

Converse with these lights

Practice this ritual until you have become able to do this while in action

EG in the shop or reading a book, it a great way to intone with another mind

Connecting two minds spell

Materials needed: Photo of the person, A candle with their favourite colour , A candle with your favourite colour , Seeds

If you would like to become better intuitive to a certain person this spell is perfect for you, soon you will be feeling what they feel and finishing their sentences.

Start by taking a picture of your chosen person and close you eyes, imagine you and them taking part in an activity together. Take candles and criss cross the wax over their picture. Still seeing your time together. Chant these words

Two minds that join as one, A unison that's ever strong

Two minds entwined our thoughts are on

Then take the photo and bury it with seeds from that persons favourite flower

An amulet to stop people intruding in your thoughts

Materials: Garlic , Basil , Sea Salt, Juniper essential oil, Small pot

There are a lot more people listening in on your mind then you realise, hundreds of thousands of people practice telepathy so its good to use a spell like this like you would a coat, if your going out in the rain, you will want some protection from catching a cold after all.

Firstly grind 3 garlic cloves, juniper essential oil, basil and sea salt . Pop it into a container like a lip balm pot or small travel pot. Carry it with you at all times you may feel venerable to physic attacks

A tip from me to enhance psychic abilities would be to drink rosemary tea with rosemary grown by your hand on your land.

Dream magic

Dream magic is the use of intentional dreaming and visualisation to achieve a desired outcome. It's a form of magic that harnesses the power of the subconscious mind to bring about change in the waking world. Dream magic can involve techniques such as lucid dreaming, dream journaling, and spell work to influence and control the contents of one's dreams. The goal is to use the dream state to explore the inner self, access hidden knowledge, and shape one's reality. However, it's important to practice dream magic ethically and responsibly, as the subconscious mind is a powerful tool that can also lead to negative consequences if used improperly. Dream spells often include herbal tea, Remember to always check with a doctor if ingredients are safe for you to personally ingest. (everyones different)

A spell to dream what you want

Materials needed: A journal or notebook , A pen ,A piece of lavender or jasmine , Your book

While in your bed, Write down your desired dream scenario in your book.

Hold the lavender or jasmine and concentrate on your intention. Chant

Dreams of magic, come to me, bring my desires, reality be

Place the journal or notebook under your pillow

Close your eyes and visualise the desired dream scenario, focusing on the feelings of excitement, joy, and positivity and drift off to sleep

A spell to heal your inner self in your sleep

Materials needed: Your book, A pen A piece of rose quartz

Write down the specific aspect of your well-being that you wish to heal. Hold the rose quartz and concentrate on your intention for healing. Repeat this chant three times:

Dreams of healing, come to me, bring my body, mind, and soul back to balance and harmony. Dreams of healing, dreams of peace, Fill me with energy and ease. May this night bring me much rest, And a feeling of being blessed.

Place the journal or notebook under your pillow. Close your eyes and visualise yourself in a peaceful, restful state, with your body, mind, and soul fully restored to health and well-being while you drift off

Prophecy dream ritual

Materials needed: lemon balm, basil, rosemary, and lavender essential oil

When we sleep is a great time to practise our craft, you don't need psychic abilities to able to have a clear prediction in your dream. In your mortar and pestle at your alter grind up basil, rosemary, lemon balm, and lavender essential oil. Speak these words

Let me see into my dreams like a window, Let me see what I demand, Let my dreams come as visions is waves

Place it into your cauldron and leave by your bed.

Dream for well being

Try this tea to gain a personal insight on your own life and achieve personal growth. Take a piece of lavender and charge it by the moons light on your alter.

Bless the lavender with this chant

take me deep within, show me what I need to see

Stir in with honey and hot water about an hour before bed

A spell for lucid dreaming

Materials needed: Lemongrass, Fresh lemon, Hot water, Purple candle

Lucid Dreaming is the practice of becoming aware of the dream state and actively manipulating the dream environment and events.

Firstly, chop up the fresh lemon and combine in a mug of hot water with the lemon grass. Find a comfortable place and light the candle. Focus on your intention to have a lucid dream. While concentrating , Chant

I can control the now I can control the later. I have power and control over my mind at all times. I can control the now and when I close my eyes I will control

the later. My dreams are mine to have and mine to control.

Drink the tea, Blow out the candle.

A spell for dreaming

Materials needed: Oats, Any herb

If your not quite sure what you want to gain from dream magic, use this spell and your dream will tell you whatever it is your destined to know. Quite simply take some fresh local herbs (homegrown is bed) and combine these in your cauldron with with oats. Take them out side to a visible moon while bare foot and chant

Moon, stars and night, Bring me sweet dreams tonight. Let me explore the wonders of my mind As I drift off to sleep and unwind

Then give your offering to nature

To remember your dream

Materials needed: Dried lavender, Chamomile , Lemon balm, Two Cups of water

Place the herbs in your cauldron and cover with the water. Chant

Goddess of the night, Bring to me the dreams of light Let me remember the

visions I see As I drift off into a dreamy sleep

Leave this on your your alter if its in your bedroom or if not leave the cauldron in your room while your sleeping.

A dream spell to ward of negativity

Materials: A white quartz crystal, White candle, Sage oil, A match

On a night you can see the moon light the candle at your alter with a match.

Focus your mind and imagine the match to be a flame that is spreading and ruining your life (this represents the negative energy) when you blow out the match imagine the negativity starting to slowly fade away. Leave the candle burning in a very safe place. Go out on in the garden , Barefoot and Take your crystal and sage oil with you. Perform a blessing on both the sage oil and crystal, then slowly put a few drops of oil onto your crystal under the moons light while chanting

I call upon the power of the light, To protect me from all that is not right

Let no harm come my way, And keep negativity at bay

Leave an offering for nature and go in to your alter and again imagine the very last thread of negativity remaining in the candle, blow out the candle imagining this is the last of all negativity

leaving your life. Sleep with the crystal
under your pillow.

Divination Magic

Divination magic is a type of magic that involves seeking knowledge through mystical means. It involves using tools, such as tarot cards, crystal balls, or astrological charts to gain insight into events that have yet to occur.

The goal of divination magic is to gain greater understanding, clarity, or guidance in a particular area of life or to make important decisions. The specific techniques and methods used can vary widely and may include the use of spells, incantations, or other forms of ritual or ceremonial magic.

In this next sub section I will guide you through my favourite forms of divination. These , for me have been the best ways to begin a journey in fortune telling. Although fortune telling can be a scary thing sometimes, so be prepared.

You may not always be told what you want to hear.

Tarot Cards

Tarot cards are a deck of 78 cards that have been used for divination and self-discovery for centuries. Each card has a unique symbolic meaning and can represent different aspects of an individual's life, including their emotions, relationships, career, and future potential. The cards are usually read in spreads, which are specific arrangements of cards that allow the reader to gain insight into a particular question or situation.

The origins of tarot cards are uncertain, with some suggesting they originated in ancient Egypt or medieval Italy. My family have always said Italy. The first recorded use of tarot cards as a divination tool was in the late 15th century in Italy, where they were used for card games . Over time, the use of tarot cards evolved into a tool for divination, and the symbols and meanings associated with each card have been passed down through generations of readers.

Each tarot deck is different, with various themes, designs, and symbolism, but they all contain the same 78 cards divided into two groups: the Major Arcana, which consists of 22 cards representing major life events, and the Minor Arcana, which consists of 56 cards that depict everyday events and experiences. They will still work as well for you no matter what design you have! But I have always found more power in an older deck of cards.

Some believe that the cards provide a way to connect with the subconscious and access deeper insights and wisdom, allowing individuals to gain clarity and make informed decisions about their lives. Others believe it is a tool for predicting the future, or rather a tool for exploring and understanding the present and potential future. You can read your own cards or someone else's. But whoever will receive the reading should shuffle the cards, and a long shuffle it should be

If you wish to explore tarot. I have laid out some of my favourite spread below.

The Celtic Cross

This spread is used for gaining an understanding of a situation or question. It involves laying out 10 cards in the following pattern

Significator: This card represents the person receiving the reading.

Crossing: This card represents the current issue or challenge.

Crowning: This card represents the influences and thoughts that are affecting the situation.

Behind: This card represents the past events that have led to the current situation.

Before: This card represents the near future and the immediate outcome of the situation.

Above: This card represents the highest aspect of the situation, such as the person's aspirations or divine guidance.

Below: This card represents the lowest aspect of the situation, such as the person's fears or limitations.

Influence from the left: This card represents the people, events, or energies that are helping the person

Influence from the right: This card represents the people, events, or energies that are hindering the person

Outcome: This card represents the final outcome of the situation.

The interpretation of the cards can vary greatly based on the reader's intuition and the context of the situation being addressed.

The Three Cross

This spread is simple and straight forward. It provides a quick overview of a situation or a question. Here's how it works:

Shuffle the deck and select three cards, laying them out left to right.

Card 1: This card represents the past and the events that have led up to the current situation.

Card 2: This card represents the present and the current situation.

Card 3: This card represents the future and the potential outcome of the situation.

The Horse Shoe

For this spread you simply lay out seven cards in a horse shoe shape.

It can be used to explore the details of any question or situation

It is often used to gain insight into a person's current state of affairs and to help form a plan of action.

Card 1: Represents past

Card 2 : Represents Present

Card 3 : Represents hidden influences

Card 4 : Represents the person asking said question

Card 5 : Represents the advice being given

Card 6 : One possible likely outcome

Card 7 : Another possible outcome or further explanation of the first outcome

Tarot Love heart

The love heart tarot card spread is a great way to gain insight into the dynamics of a relationship. It consists of seven cards laid out in the shape of a heart. The first card is placed at the centre and represents the relationship as a whole. The other six cards are placed around it, each representing an aspect of the relationship. Whoever is having there cards read should write out the number 1-6 and pick a relationship aspect of reach number ie 1) trust 2) commitment 3) Longevity Etc.

This is a great way to use tarot cards to help a person in the love life.

Tarot Star

This is a spread used throughout the south of the uk for a very long time. Another self lead spread. It's a great way to gain insight into a particular situation or question. It consists of nine cards laid out in the shape of a star.

The first card is placed at the centre and represents the core of the situation.

 The person that is having there cards read should write down numbers 1-8 on a piece of paper and pick a subject for there situation.

Ie 1) Obstacles I will face 2) Advice 3) Opportunities etc

To read the cards, start by looking at the central card and interpreting its meaning. Then look at each of the eight surrounding cards and interpret their meanings in relation to the central card. This will give you insight into how all the different aspects of your situation interact with each other.

Self lead spread are very good for a more personalised tarot card reading in relation to the person having there cards read.

Reading tea leaves

Tea leaf reading is an ancient way of fortune-telling that first originated in China, where tea drinkers interpreted the various shapes of tea leaves left at the bottom of the cup. Spreading around the rest of the world over time, alot of elder witches will read tea leaves as easy as me and you may read a magazine article.

You can use wine sediments, coffee grounds or tea leaves.

The allure of this form of prophecy is that it does not require specialised tools. Therefore, it is not only an economical form of divination, but also an low-profile method.

I would recommend to use rough loose tea with wide leaves, as the chunks are larger and tend to stick to the sides and bottom of the cup.

It is traditional to use a teacup and saucer. You should use a tea cup that is wide with slanted side.
The shape of the teacup makes it easy for the tea leaves to form different configurations.

To prepare the tea, pour hot water into the cup first adding in your tea leaves after. As you drink, Focus on questions and keep your intentions at the forefront. When you have a small mouth full of tea left over in the cup , swish the cup around three times clockwise. Put the saucer on top of the cup. Then turn the cup and saucer upside down to drain the remaining water into the saucer. Wait a minute then turn the mug back round the right way , then look for patterns the tea leaves have given.

So how do you read the patterns?
Firstly it takes a lot of initiative.

You have to follow both your gut and your head and go with the flow with what you feel when you see the leaves. Practice will make perfect with this craft. Keep in mind that reading tea leaves is a personal and intuitive practice, and there is no one right way to do it.

A heart shape obviously indicates love

A ring shape can symbolise a wedding or commitment such as a business deal

A ladder shape can suggest progress or upward movement

A cross shape may indicate obstacles or challenges to overcome.

A triangle shape can symbolise good luck or success.

A broken line or a scattered pattern can indicate a sense of fragmentation or disconnection

A star shape can represent hope, inspiration, or good fortune

A Tree means Growth, stability, and good health

The Butterfly stands for Transformation, change, and metamorphosis

Spider represents Creativity and the ability to manifest one's desires

A boat represents Journey, travel, and adventure

The sun shows Success, happiness, and positive energy

A moon shape shows Emotions, intuition, and mystery

If your reading someone else's leaves, you will need to find out some of the happenings in there day to day life to better unstained their leaves.

Astragalomancy

Astragalomancy , other wise known as dice magic is a form of fortune telling that uses small objects, such as bones and dice, to predict the future.

The practice originated in ancient civilisations and was used to answer questions or make decisions.

The word "astragalomancy" comes from the Greek word "astragalos," which refers to a knuckle bone.

To perform astragalomancy, the objects are thrown or cast, and the way they fall or the pattern they form is interpreted to give insight into the future.

The interpretation of the results can vary depending on the specific culture and tradition, So this is a general method of reading the dice.

Obviously in this day and age we are not using bones so I rely solely on dice.

So essentially the practice involves rolling two dice and interpreting the results based on their numerical value and the particular arrangement of them. The arrangement of the dice is said to represent different aspects of one's life, and the interpretation of the results is thought to give insight into the future. The person who is having their dice read should be the personal to shake the dice before in their hand.

There is a huge range of dice on the market in regards to divination so start of with normal board game dice then treat your self to a divination dice, they're great!

Simple three dice roll

Meditate and clear your mind. Ask the dice three yes or no questions of your choice then roll.

Odds are No

Evens are Yes

Read the dice from left to right in order of questions. If they land in a triangle shape its a sign of a bad omen. If they land in a straight line it shows positive change.

Circle dice roll

Take six dice. Create a circle about 30cm round on a table. Take the dice and grip them in your hand, Clear your mind consider the circumstance for which you are seeking advice. When you feel ready, throw the dice. When you do roll the dice do not try to influence it to stay in the circle. Roll it true to your heart or else they would be no point in doing this.

If they fall out of the circle

One dice - You will face difficulties

Two dice - You will face disputes

Three dice - Anxiety and tress

Any more than three dice out of the circle is considered a very bad omen. Any dice that fall on the floor can be seen as a sign of good luck.

Any dice that fall with in the circle signify good fortune and your situation planning out the way you hope, so if you end up with six dice in the circle, good for you! If not, maybe avoid the plan you had made.

Bag of dice

Take a bag full of dice. Clear you mind, centre yourself and think of a question, reach in and pull out a random amount of dice.

Roll them out and count how many pulled out. The number of dice pulled will determine your answer.

Even numbers mean yes and odd numbers mean no.

The Crystal Ball

The use of crystal balls for fortune telling has a long history, with roots in ancient cultures such as the Celts, Greeks, and Romans.

The practice of scrying, or divination through gazing into a transparent object, dates back thousands of years and was used to communicate with the spirit world. In the Middle Ages, crystal balls were used by alchemists and mystics. The idea of using a crystal ball for fortune telling became very popular in the Victorian era, when spiritualism and interest in the supernatural rose. A skilled practitioner could possibly use a crystal ball to see into the future, communicate with the dead, or gain insight into the unknown.

Even today, crystal balls are still used as a tool for divination. Remember, most mystics do not walk around telling every body they are a mystic, so a lot more people then you might suspect could be using a crystal ball.

The use of crystal balls for fortune telling remains a personal and subjective practice, and the interpretation of the images and impressions received during a scrying session will vary from person to person.

Crystal balls are harder to obtain then maybe they were 100 years ago, but you can still get them at an affordable price. Of course as always check second hand online marketplaces.

If you have never use this method before, like all things, practice makes perfect so don't be disheartened if you do nor get it right first time.

I would advice using dream and physic magic for a while before trying this to help become more intone with your inner mystic.

So how do we read a crystal ball? Choose a quiet, dimly lit room where you won't be disturbed. Light candles or incense, and cleanse the crystal ball by holding it under running water or smudging it with sage.

Sit comfortably and hold the crystal ball in your hands, focusing your energy into it. Visualise your intention for the scrying session, such as seeking insight or communicating with a spirit guide.

Stare into the crystal ball, allowing your gaze to soften and your mind to become relaxed. Let your eyes go out of focus, and allow any images or impressions to come to you naturally.

Observe the shapes, colours, and movements within the crystal ball. Interpret the images or impressions that come to you, and try to understand their meaning.

Keep a record: It's helpful to keep a journal or record of your scrying sessions, so you can refer back to them later and see if patterns or themes emerge over time.

If you are trying to communicate with a spirit guide using the ball, the premise is essentially the same. The only alteration is that instead of reading an outcome from the ball itself, you call out to the spirit realm for guidance and then proceed to read the ball after you feel as though the barrier between the earthly and sprit realm has broken.

In Conclusion

And so, this spell book comes to a close, I can only wish this book has served as some help to you.

These spells come from my heart and the world over.

Magic is a timeless and powerful force that has been woven into the fabric of humanity for centuries.

This book has provided a glimpse into the vast and diverse world of magic, offering a range of spells, rituals, and practices that have been proven to be effective.

However, always remember that magic is always within you. The spells contained within these pages are but a mere guide to tap into the power you already possess.

Trust in your intuition and the universe, for the magic you seek is within reach. So, go forth, light the candles, mix the ingredients, and cast the spells. The magic is yours to command. Blessed be.

Printed in Great Britain
by Amazon

54471904R00085